*For Harry Weinman,
my terrific Uncle Ned,
with gratitude*

Jason Everett Bear and his mother lived in a tidy little house deep in the forest. They took long walks under the trees and had long talks in the kitchen, and they loved each other.

And there was someone else Jason loved. Himself.

"I'm terrific," he told himself over and over. "And I do terrific things."

Jason had a big box of gold stars.

Every time he did something terrific, he gave himself a star.

Or very terrific. Two stars.

Occasionally he gave himself three stars. Super terrific.

Jason's tongue was always gummy from licking so many stars. But that didn't keep him from talking. "When I hear myself talk I always hear wonderful things," he said to himself.

One day his neighbor, Raymond Squirrel, came by. Jason was sweeping the front steps. "I'm a terrific worker," Jason said. "I work so hard that some days my mother has nothing to do but look at her toenails and eat chocolates."

"Ridiculous," said Raymond.

"Also, I never wipe dirt on towels," said Jason.

"You're boring," said Raymond. "I bet you eat spinach, too."

"Of course," said Jason. "My mother mixes it with white sauce and calls it Green Cloud Supreme, and I eat it all up."

"Yecch!" cried Raymond. And he went away.

"Raymond doesn't understand," said Jason. And he swept his steps with all his strength. Then he stood back to admire them. "A neat job. Maybe a two-star job."

Jason sat down on his clean steps to rest. Along came Marvin Raccoon.

"Want to see the cleanest steps in the forest?" asked Jason.

"Not if I can help it," said Marvin, and he started to walk away.

"Stay and talk for awhile," said Jason. "Here. Have a clean seat."

"No thanks," said Marvin. And he started to walk away again.

"Wait," said Jason. "Why are you going away? Is there something wrong with me?"

"Hah!" said Marvin.

"If I asked you to name ten things about me, would nine of them be good?"

"You must be joking," said Marvin.

"My mother says I'm a good bear," said Jason.

"You're a mama's bear," said Marvin, and he walked away.

Jason sat alone on his clean steps. "Sometimes when somebody knows you for a long time, they don't appreciate you," he told himself. "Except maybe mothers."

One day a new bear moved into the forest.

"I'm going out to make a new friend," Jason told his mother.

"Here's my chance for someone new to appreciate me," Jason told himself.

Jason went over to introduce himself.

"I'm Jason Everett Bear," he said. "I suppose you've heard of me."

"I'm Henrietta Emily Bear, and I haven't."

Henrietta looked closely at Jason. "Why should I have heard of you?"

"Well," said Jason, "the truth is that I'm terrific. And I do terrific things."

"Name one."

"See my shiny hair?" said Jason. "I brush it till it squeaks. Brush your hair twice a day, and all the knots will go away. I am also industrious, lovable and——"

"A show-off!" said Henrietta. And she slammed the door.

"You have a very bad disposition," Jason said to the door, and then he walked home.

Jason went to bed early. He always went to bed early. "Eight hours of rest puts hair on my chest."

But Jason couldn't sleep. The next morning he said to his mother, "Maybe I'm not terrific after all."

"Oh?"

"You're the only one left who thinks I'm terrific. Maybe I'm just a mama's bear." Jason looked at his mother. "I want to be my own bear," he said.

"That's what I want you to be," said Mrs. Bear. "As you grow up, you will try new things. You will learn what's right for you, and what isn't right for you. Then you will be your own bear."

"Lately I haven't tried anything new," said Jason. "I'm tired of the same old stuff. I'm ready for something different."

"Fine," said Mrs. Bear.

"I'm not going to clean the house or me any-more," said Jason.

"All right," said Mrs. Bear.

"I'll be so dirty that flies and bugs will crawl all over me."

"Flies and bugs have rights," said Mrs. Bear.

"The piles of garbage will reach the ceiling and make funny marks on it," said Jason. "And we will have to wear clothespins on our noses."

"I have a couple of clothespins I can spare," said Mrs. Bear.

"I'm also going to clobber Richy Ratfink today," said Jason.

"He probably deserves it," said Mrs. Bear.

"I'm finished with spinach," said Jason.

"It's getting out of season anyway," said Mrs. Bear.

"I'm a brand-new bear," said Jason. "And now I'm going to try out the new me."

"Good luck, dear," said Mrs. Bear.

Jason went over to Marvin's house.

Marvin was in bed.

"Good morning, good morning," said Jason. "I want you to be the second to know."

"The second to know what?" asked Marvin, opening one eye.

"The new me," said Jason.

"Oh?" said Marvin. He opened his other eye. "What's new about you?"

"I've stopped eating spinach," said Jason.

"You don't say," said Marvin. And he closed one eye.

"I've stopped cleaning the house."

"Really?" said Marvin. And he closed the other eye.

"How can you sleep at a time like this?" said Jason. Jason bent over Marvin and very carefully tied knots all over Marvin's fur. He tied big knots, little knots, fancy knots and plain knots.

Then Jason stepped back and admired his work. "Three-star knots," he said.

"What?" said Marvin, opening his eyes. He
looked at himself. "Knots!" he cried. "I'm covered
with knots!"

"*I* did it! I *did* it!" said Jason.

"Untie me," said Marvin. "Untie me this instant."

"I don't untie. I only tie. That's the new me,"
said Jason. And he left.

Jason went to Raymond's house. Raymond was
outside gathering nuts.

"Look at me," said Jason.

"I'm looking," said Raymond.

"Well?"

"Well what?" asked Raymond, as he put his nuts into little piles.

"I'm different," said Jason.

"Than what?" asked Raymond.

"Than I was," said Jason. "I save garbage, I attract flies, I tie knots."

Raymond continued to pile his nuts.

"There's something else different about me," said Jason. "I kick nut piles." And Jason quickly knocked down all of Raymond's piles.

"A two-star kick," said Jason.

"Hey, pick those up," said Raymond.

"The new me doesn't pick up. It only knocks down," said Jason. And he ran off.

Jason went to Henrietta's house.

"I'm a new bear," he said.

"Really?" said Henrietta.

"I tied Marvin's fur in knots. I kicked Raymond's piles of nuts. I'm going to clobber Richy Ratfink. I'm going to stuff cement into toothpaste tubes."

"Show-off!" said Henrietta. And she slammed the door.

"You don't like me," Jason said to the door.

Jason walked away. He sat down by a stream and felt sad. "Nobody thinks the new me is terrific. So maybe it's not."

Jason ran back to Marvin's house. "I'm sorry for what the new me did," he said. And he untied Marvin.

Jason went to Raymond's house. "Please forgive the new me," he said, as he piled up the nuts.

He went to Henrietta's house. But she didn't
answer the door. He left a flower, and then he
went home.

His mother was sitting on the porch. "Nobody likes the new me," he said, "and neither do I." Jason sat down beside his mother. "Now I don't know who I am."

"I know who you are," said Mrs. Bear. "You are a good bear who is thinking things over."

"Well, that is a good thing to be," said Jason. "A thinking bear."

Jason spent the rest of the day thinking. "This is the first real thinking I have done in a long time. I am out of practice. I hope I don't make a mistake."

Jason went to bed thinking. The next morning he woke up and ran downstairs shouting, "Mother, I am what I am. I am Jason Everett Bear, and I'm glad of it."

Jason's mother hugged him. "I am glad, too," she said.

"I don't need stars or clean steps or cement toothpaste or knots or anything," said Jason, and he ran back upstairs to his room. He opened his big box of gold stars. He ripped stars from his walls, lampshades, tables, chairs, bureau and bed.

He took all his stars outside. He put up a sign in his yard: GIANT GIVE-AWAY, STARS, NEW AND USED.

Henrietta, Marvin and Raymond came along. "What are you doing?" they asked.

"I am giving away my stars," said Jason. "I don't need them anymore."

"I don't believe it," said Marvin.

"Believe it. Believe it," said Jason.

"What about the old you and the new you?" asked Henrietta.

"Who are they?" asked Jason. "I am simply Jason Everett Bear. I have nothing more to say."

"Incredible," said Raymond.
"Fantastic," said Marvin.

"Terrific," said Henrietta.
"Thank you," said Jason.